For

Anna Sujatha Mathai

and Rahul, Nakul and Nisha

VIKING
Published by the Penguin Group
Penguin Books Ltd, 27 Wrights Lane, London W8 5TZ, England
Penguin Books USA Inc., 375 Hudson Street, New York, New York 10014, USA
Penguin Books Australia Ltd, Ringwood, Victoria, Australia
Penguin Books Canada Ltd, 10 Alcorn Avenue, Toronto, Ontario, Canada M4V 3B2
Penguin Books (NZ) Ltd, 182–190 Wairau Road, Aukland 10, New Zealand

Penguin Books Registered Offices: Harmondsworth, Middlesex, England

First Published 1992
1 3 5 7 9 10 8 6 4 2

Text copyright © Akumal Ramachander, 1992
Illustrations copyright © Stasys Eidrigevicius, 1992

Photography by Krzysztof Szeloch

Filmset in Monophoto Perpetua
Made and Printed in Hong Kong by Imago Publishing Limited

A CIP catalogue record for this book is available from the British Library

ISBN 0–670–84350–4

LITTLE PIG

AKUMAL RAMACHANDER

ILLUSTRATED BY
STASYS EIDRIGEVICIUS

VIKING

Little Pig was born to Mama Pig and Papa Pig on Mary's Pig Farm. Mary bred pigs on her farm and when they got big and round and fat she would wait for the first Monday of the month. On this day a van would arrive on her farm. The appearance of the van was not always a good sign for the pigs. They felt that somehow the van cut short their stay on Mary's farm and things would never be the same again.

When Little Pig was born, he looked very pretty. Mary felt she had never seen such a charming little one on her farm. She fell in love with Little Pig and decided to build a separate house for him. Little Pig had a special bed, a nice chair to sit on and even a breakfast bowl for his cereal every morning.

Whenever Mary returned home from shopping, she would have presents for Little Pig. Sometimes Mary ran into problems – not all the stores had clothes for baby pigs.

Mary also taught Little Pig various tricks. Little Pig could ride a bicycle, play with a ball and even play the piano.

People who lived near Mary's farm watched all this with utter fascination. They had never seen anything quite like this before. They nicknamed Little Pig "Mary's Little Lamb". In fact he *was* Mary's little lamb. Little Pig went wherever Mary went, especially when she hummed a particular tune which he loved.

But as months passed, Little Pig started
to grow up.

Every month the van arrived at Mary's farm.
The driver would pack his van with pigs and
drive away, leaving some pigs frightened and
Little Pig confused.

One day Little Pig saw the van parked in front
of Mary's house as usual, and he found
something strange happening. Mama Pig and
Papa Pig were being dragged into the van by
the driver, and Mary was giving him a helping
hand. Before Little Pig could shout "Hey!
Stop! You can't do that to my Mama and
Papa!" the van had disappeared.

That evening Little Pig felt very sad. Mary noticed Little Pig's sorrow but she could not cheer him up. She knew that he, too, had to leave the farm one day.

Soon Little Pig realized that Mary's feelings towards him had changed. But Little Pig just felt puzzled. He still loved Mary. He didn't understand why Mary had stopped loving him. Now Little Pig started to have strange dreams every night – dreams about fierce-looking drivers in mysterious vans.

One day when Little Pig woke up, he found
the van right in front of his house. Little Pig
came out to see what was happening. As soon
as the driver saw Little Pig he ran to
catch him, but Little Pig just moved
a few paces away. The driver fell on his face,
shrieking, and cursed Little Pig. Then a chase began.
The driver pounced on Little Pig and tried his best
to grab him and push him into the van. But
Little Pig escaped every time.

Mary, who had been watching them,
decided to act.

She started humming a tune – the very tune
that Little Pig loved. Little Pig stopped in his
tracks. He hadn't heard that tune for a long
time. Little Pig began to follow Mary, and
Mary went round and round her house with
Little Pig trotting behind her. Then she turned
around, all of a sudden, and jumped into the
van. Little Pig just followed her into the van,
wagging his tail.

Then suddenly, in a flash, Mary jumped out of
the van and helped the driver bang the door

shut.

Little Pig was shocked! He was now trapped —
trapped with all those Mama Pigs, Papa Pigs
and Little Pigs. Little Pig realized he was no
longer special. He shared the same fate as all
the other pigs bred and reared on Mary's farm.
His future seemed to vanish altogether from his
sight.

The driver drove away in the heat of the
afternoon, pleased that he had a van
full of pigs.

After driving for a couple of hours, the driver stopped near a roadside café to have a drink. Parked nearby was a bus of young school children.

Hearing grunts coming from the van, some of the children wanted to find out what was making all the noise. One of them very bravely opened the door of the van to take a good look. And before he could say "Porky Pig!" the pigs, led by Little Pig, jumped out of the van and plunged into the fields nearby. In a moment they had all vanished from sight.

When the driver returned, he found the door still open. It didn't take him long to realize it was an empty van he had to drive back.

That night, Mary felt uneasy. She
remembered how she had tricked poor,
unsuspecting Little Pig into the van. As she fell
fast asleep, she had a terrible dream in which
she saw Little Pig escape with all the other
pigs, and march on her farm. Mary saw
hundreds of pigs pointing accusingly at her,
telling her what a nasty woman she was. Little
Pig kept on asking Mary: "Why did you trick
me? How could you deceive someone whom
you loved? How could you betray a pig? What
if *you* were one?"

Then Mary felt something weird happen to her.
She felt she was slowly turning into a pig! She
woke up, startled, and then went back to
sleep. There was nothing wrong with her.
It was just a dream.

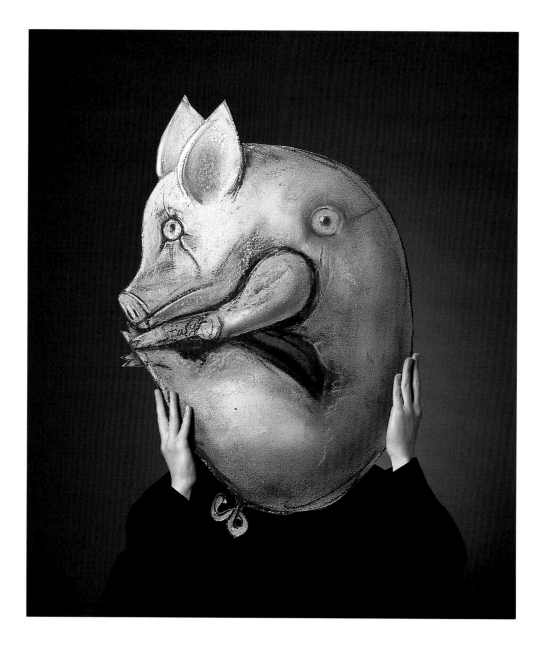

The next morning the van arrived in front of Mary's house. The driver yelled, "Mary, come here; something awful happened yesterday. Someone let all the pigs escape."

The driver was horrified when he saw a pig come out of the house dressed in Mary's clothes. He knew he wasn't drunk, but he had never seen a pig dressed in a woman's clothes before! Since he didn't have much time to think, he just bundled Mary into the van and drove off, relieved that he was not driving back an empty van this time.